LAURA OWEN & KORKY PAUL

Winnie AND Wilbur

WINNIE
Takes the
Plunge

OXFORD
UNIVERSITY PRESS

CONTENTS

WINNIE'S
Mouse Organ

WINNIE
takes the Plunge

Supersize
SURPRISE

'Hoo-bloomingray!' sang Winnie. 'It's the fancy dress party today!'

Winnie and Wilbur were taking a basket of food to the school ready for the party. They had pickle buns, and sandwiches with real sand in them.

'We've all got to dress up,' said Winnie. 'You can be Puss in Boots, Wilbur, and I'll be . . .' But Winnie wasn't looking where she was going.

Trip-crash!

'Oi!' said Winnie. 'What's that
blooming log ... er ... leg ... doing
across the path?'

A muffled sound of deep sobbing came
from the bushes beside the path.

Sob!

'Jerry?' said Winnie. 'Is that you?'

Sniff! 'Yes, missus,' said Jerry.

Winnie pushed through the bush.

'What in the whoopsy-world is up with you?' said Winnie.

'It's just—sniff—that there's a party . . . !'

'I know!' said Winnie. 'Everyone's invited!'

'. . . except me!' said Jerry.

'Why's that, then?' said Winnie.

9

'Cos I is a giant!' said Jerry.
'Everybody's read giant stories
in books, and now they think all
giants is 'orrible. That's why I'm
not invited!'

'Rubbish bins!' said Winnie. 'There are
some lovely stories about giants. There's
that nice one about Jack climbing up the
beansprout where he meets a giant who . . .
ooer. Well, there's that one about the
Shellfish Giant who doesn't let the
children . . . oh. I do see what you mean,
Jerry!' said Winnie. 'But that's just
blooming stories, not real life and people
like us!'

'Then how come nobody ever
wants to play with me?' said Jerry.

10

'Wilbur and I will!' said Winnie. 'Come
on, let's play hide and sneak. Go and hide,
Jerry. I'll count to a hundred, then I'll
come and find you.'

'Goody!' smiled Jerry, and off he went—thump, thump, thump!

Winnie began to count.

'One nitty-gnat, two nitty-gnat, three nitty-gnat . . .'

Thump, thump, thump!

'Go quietly!' shouted Winnie. 'I can hear where you are! Twenty-two nitty-gnat, twenty- . . .'

Tiptoe-crash! Tiptoe-crack!

'Ninety-eight nitty-gnat, ninety-nine nitty gnat, *one hundred!*' shouted Winnie. 'Coming, ready-steady or not!'

Winnie opened her eyes . . . and saw
Jerry's bottom sticking right out of the
smelly-berry bush . . . just at the same
moment as a little girl saw it, and . . .

Shriek! 'Where'th my Mumumummy?'
shouted the little girl.

'Er, found you, Jerry!' said Winnie.

'See, missus!' said Jerry. 'See?
I ain't no good at playing!
And I frighten people!'

13

'You've turned hide and sneak into hide and shriek!' said Winnie. 'Let's try leapfrog instead!'

Thump-bump! went Winnie as she tried to leap over Jerry but leapt into him instead. **Splat!** went Wilbur. Jerry was just too big for them to get over.

'Oo, I'm as puffed as popcorn and as bruised as a boomerang banana!' said Winnie. 'I give up!'

'See?' said Jerry. 'See?'

'Yes, I do see,' said Winnie. 'But don't
you worry, Jerry! You *shall* go to the party!'

Wilbur found an idea in a book of photos.
It showed a street party from the olden days.

'Perfect!' said Winnie. 'Quick! I must
phone Mrs Parmar!'

Down on the High Street, Winnie waved her wand. 'Abracadabra!'

Instantly there was a ring road to take all the cars away from the village. 'We need party decorations,' said Winnie. She waved her wand. 'Abracadabra!' And there were flowers. 'I'll just put them in pots,' said Winnie. She jumped

onto her broom and flew up onto the roof tops, stopping to poke flowers into all the chimney pots. 'As pretty as a pink cockroach!' she said. Then Winnie flew around, scooping up washing lines from back gardens to drape them from the lamp posts. 'Big bloomers bunting!' she said.

17

Down below, Mrs Parmar was sorting the tables and chairs and food and drink.

'Where can we put Jerry?' said Mrs Parmar. 'He'd break any of these ordinary chairs!'

'Leave it to me, Mrs P!' said Winnie. '*Abracadabra!*'

Instantly there was a giant throne of a chair. And there was a hole in the ground so that Jerry's chair could be sunk down and be at the right height for him to use the same table as everyone else.

'Well done, Winnie!' said Mrs Parmar.
She laid Jerry a place with a dustbin lid
plate and a bucket cup.

'Here they all come!' said Mrs Parmar.
'We'll have party games first, then tea.
Oh, but we're not dressed-up, Winnie!'

'Easy-peasy tight pants squeezy!' said
Winnie. She waved her wand.
'Abradacabra!'

19

Don't Winnie and Mrs Parmar look
lovely?

Mrs Parmar announced the first party
game.

'Hide and Seek!'

'Dear, oh dear, Wilbur!' said Winnie.
'How's Jerry going to get on? Where is he,
anyway?'

Wilbur shrugged.

The children hid here and there, and
just about everywhere. Some of them
chose to hide in a tree. They climbed up
into its branches, then they sat and waited
to be found.

'I like it up here!' said one child.

'So do I,' said another, 'Did you know that Jerry the giant is coming to the party?'

The tree quivered.

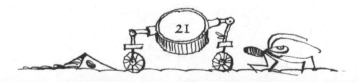

'Is he?' said a third child. 'Oh, good! I like Jerry.'

'So do I!' said both the other children. Then—**splash!**—'What's that?' said the first one. 'It's raining inside this tree!'

But it wasn't rain. It was Jerry.

'Sniff!' went the tree.

'Jerry?' said Winnie. 'Is that you?'

'It is, missus!' said Jerry. **'I is crying because I is so happy!'**

22

'Jerry's costume wins the fancy dress competition!' said Mrs Parmar. 'He's a wonderful tree! He gets a book for his prize.'

'Oo, just a moment, Mrs P,' said Winnie when she saw the book in Mrs Parmar's hand. She waved her wand. 'Abracadabra!'

Instantly the book changed.

'Is it a book about giants?' asked Jerry, looking worried.

'Yes, but NICE giants!' said Winnie.

'Ooo,' said Jerry, and he hugged the book hard.

Jerry let the children climb all over him, and he swung them round.

Then, 'Shall we play leapfrog?' said
Winnie.

'But ...!' began Jerry.

'Don't worry!' said Winnie. She waved
her wand. 'Abracadabra!'

And instantly all the children had froggy legs and froggy feet. They could leap over Jerry with no trouble at all.

Leap! Leap! Leap!

But when it was Jerry's turn to leap over the children, they all collapsed!

'Time for tea!' said Mrs Parmar.

They ate and they talked. Then they filled the hole in the ground with water, and the children went swimming with their froggy legs which made them swim extra fast!

And guess what? When Jerry got home he found an invitation stuck in his letter box. He'd been invited to the party all along, but just didn't know it!

'You silly great lummox!' said Winnie.

28

The Abominable
WINNIE!

Winnie looked out of the window and
squealed.

'Yippeee-dippeee, Wilbur! There's
snow as deep as a maggoty-mallow pie!'

Winnie went down to the kitchen and
made a big blubbling bucket of grey
splorridge. She dolloped the splorridge
into mini cauldrons, then dribbled it with
snail syrup.

'Mmmm!' said Winnie. Sniff! 'That
smells truly abominable!'

29

'Meeow?' asked Wilbur, licking syrup off his spoon.

'D'you like that word—abominable?' said Winnie. 'I'm not completely absolutely sure what it means, but I have been told that my cooking is abominable.' **Lick! Slurp!**

'**Yum!** So abominable must mean really, really, really nice, mustn't it?'

'Meeow!' Wilbur shook his head and pointed towards a dictionary, but Winnie was looking out of the window.

'Let's go out and play!'

They put on hats and gloves and tail warmers, and went out into the cold.

'Watch this!' said Winnie. **Splodge!**
She tipped herself over into the snow to
make a witch-shaped print. It was a bit
messy.

Splat! Wilbur made a cat print that
was crisp and clean. He added twigs for
whiskers.

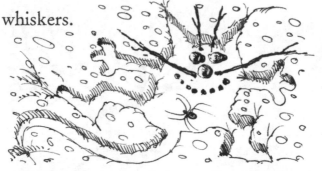

'I s'ppose yours is better!' said Winnie.
They made an ice slide, and slid along it
with their arms out to help them balance

Wheeeeeeee-bump! went Winnie.

Wheeeeeeeeeeeeeeee! went
Wilbur, going much further.

'Huh!' said Winnie, rubbing her bottom.
'Snowball fights are what I'm really really—
abominably—good at. Watch this!' Winnie
scooped up snow and squashed it into
a ball. She threw the snowball at
Wilbur—*splat!*

'Splat on the cat!' said Winnie. 'Hee hee!'

Plop! Wilbur threw one back, and soon they were having a snowball fight.

Chuck! went Winnie. **Splat!**

'Hit!'

'Mrrrow!'

Throw! went Wilbur. **Duck!** went Winnie.

'Missed!' shouted Winnie.

Then Wilbur scooped a really big
snowball and threw it—**pheeeew-plop!**
to land wetly and coldly right down
Winnie's neck.

'Urgh!' shouted Winnie. 'Ooo, you
meany, Wilbur! That was horrible.'

'Meeheehee!' laughed Wilbur.

'Stop it!' said Winnie. 'Or I'm not playing with you any more!'

But Wilbur threw another snowball that landed—*splat!*—right in Winnie's face.

'Meeheehee!'

'Right!' said Winnie. 'You're not my friend any more, Wilbur the cat!'

Winnie stomped off to where the children were making snowmen.

'Can I help?' asked Winnie.

She added this . . . and that . . . and those
to make the snowman more special. 'Good,
isn't it!' said Winnie.

'Look at that one!' laughed the children.
They were pointing to where Wilbur had
made another snowman. 'It's a snow witch!
Snow Winnie! Ha ha!'

'Huh!' said Winnie. 'I can make our snowman better than that one! Shall I?'

'Yes, please!' said the children.

'I'll make it into an abominable snowman!' said Winnie. She waved her wand.

'Abracadabra!'

'Uh-oh!' said the children. 'W-w-what's that?'

'A lovely abominable snowman, that's what,' said Winnie. 'A really nice big . . . Er, it really is very very big, isn't it!'

Gulp! went the children.

The abominable snowman was *huge!* It was hairy. And it was moving! It was taking great big footsteps towards them, and it didn't look friendly! **Thump-thump!**

38

'Er, hello, nice Mr Abominable!' said Winnie.

THUMP-THUMP!

'Heck in a hairnet, run!' shouted
Winnie. Winnie and the children began
to run down the hill, but the abominable
snowman was running even faster after
them.

Thump-thump-thump!

'He's going to catch us!' said Winnie.

Dive! Wilbur threw himself at the
abominable snowman, trying to stop it.
But the abominable snowman just tripped
over Wilbur and began to roll down the
hill, roly-poly faster and faster, turning
itself into a giant snowball.

Rumble-roll!

41

'*Abraca*——!' began Winnie. But
splat-gulp! Winnie was rolled into the
ball that was growing bigger and bigger as it
picked up more snow. The abominable
snowball began to pick up children too.
Splat-gulp! Splat-gulp!

Then, 'Leave those children alone, you
great bully!' shouted Mrs Parmar. She
stepped into the path of the abominable
snowman that had turned into an
abominable snowball. She held up a hand—

'Stop!' she commanded. But the
abominable snowball scooped up
Mrs Parmar, too.

Luckily the hill flattened out, so the
abominable snowball rolled to a halt. There
were arms, legs and heads sticking out of it.

'Frosted fidgets!' said Winnie. 'Where's my wand?' Wilbur ran up and handed her the wand. She just managed to wave it. *Abracadabra!*

Ppffuff! The snowball gently exploded, spilling Winnie and children and Mrs Parmar into the snow. The abominable snowman snowball was gone.

'Thank snow goosey-ganders for that!' said Winnie. She tried to stand up, but fell straight over because she was so dizzy from rolling. But she was smiling. 'Eee, I've just had a blooming brilliant idea!' she said.

44

'Oh dear,' said dizzy Mrs Parmar.

'We should make a really big snow ball!' said Winnie.

'Absolutely *not* another one!' said Mrs Parmar. 'We've all had quite enough of big snowballs for one day.'

'Not a snowball, Mrs P!' said Winnie. 'A Snow Ball! You know, with dancing and posh frocks and bow ties and music and all that!'

But Mrs Parmar was still shaking her head. 'We couldn't possibly organize a snow ball by this evening. There isn't time to make food and buy dresses and . . .'

'Just look over there, everybody!' said Winnie. All the heads turned, and Winnie gave a quick whisk of her wand. '*Abracadabra!*'

'Wow!'

Instantly there was a sparkling snow
dome made from the abominable
snowball's snow. An igloo ballroom!
And everyone was dressed for a ball.
There was a band. And food. And balloons.

Doo-be-doo-wap-wap! The music
started.

'Ahem, meeeow!'

'Wilbur!' said Winnie. 'Oh, you look so dashing! And you were so brave, trying to save us from that abominable snowman!'

'Meeow!' said Wilbur modestly.

'Oh, Wilbur, I'm sorry I was as moody as a mouldy melon earlier!' said Winnie. 'Please, can we be friends again?'

'Meeow!' grinned Wilbur. He held up
one front leg.

'Ooo, yes! I'd love to dance with you!'
said Winnie.

So Winnie and Wilbur, and Mrs Parmar
and all the children, danced as the night
grew dark outside. They danced as the sun
began to rise and warm the world, and the
igloo ballroom began to drip.

Everyone was hot from dancing.

'*Abracadabra!*' said Winnie, and suddenly the snow of the ballroom turned into red and orange and green and purple ice-lollies.

'Have a lick!' said Winnie.

Winnie licked green gherkin lolly while Wilbur munched on a golden kipper-flavoured chunk.

'You know what, Wilbur?' said Winnie. 'That was an abominable party!'

'You're wrong, Winnie!' said Mrs Parmar. 'Abominable means terrible.'

'Does it?' said Winnie.

'And that party was wonderful!'

'So my abominable cooking is . . .'

'Interesting,' said Mrs Parmar firmly. 'Goodbye!'

WINNIE'S
Mouse Organ

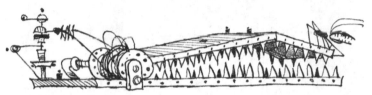

Pong! Phew!

Winnie and Wilbur were flying along with pegs on their noses because they'd got some lumps of the smelliest green hairy mouldy cheese in their basket.

'This will tempt those blooming noisy mice out!' said Winnie. 'I'll put it in the crocodile jaw trap, and it can **snip-snap** them up, and then tonight we can sleep! We won't be woken by their blooming scratching and squeaking ever again!'

Then, 'Ooo, look at that, Wilbur!' said
Winnie. There was a poster outside the
school. 'Just look at that shiny snaily
thingy! And a great big nappy pin!
Whatever are they?'

Mrs Parmar was coming out of the
school.

Sniff! 'What's that ghastly smell?' she asked.

'Just cheese,' said Winnie. 'Do you want to try some?'

'No thank you!' said Mrs Parmar. 'Ah! I see that you're looking at our poster. We are hoping to enthuse the children with a love of music.'

'Coo!' said Winnie. 'I'm enthused already! I'd love to play one of those funny things!'

'Well,' said Mrs Parmar. 'If you could play an instrument, you would be more than welcome at school this afternoon. So far we haven't been able to find a musician to come and play for us.'

'Ooo, I'll volunteer, Mrs P!' said Winnie. 'I'll show the little ordinaries how to make lovely music!'

'Mrrrow!' Wilbur dropped his head into his paws.

'Which instrument do you play?' asked
Mrs Parmar.

'Oh,' said Winnie. 'It's . . . er . . . um.
Well, you'll just have to wait and see,
Mrs P. But I'll be along later with my
ninstrument, don't you worry!'

'Well, thank you!' said Mrs Parmar.
'I'll tell the head teacher right away!'

'Wow-zow!' said Winnie, as they
flew home. 'Ooo, lovely-dovely
brillaramaroodles! I'm going to be
a musician!'

'Meeeow?' asked Wilbur.

'How?' said Winnie. 'Easy-peasy
turnip-juice-squeezy! I just need a
ninstrument and then I'll play it.'

Back home, Winnie waved her wand.
'Abracadabra!'

And instantly, there at Winnie's feet
was something that looked like a hairy
beast with spikes.

'Hisss!' went Wilbur.

'It's a blagpipe!' said Winnie. 'Just you
listen to this!' Winnie blew down a pipe.
Up plumped the hairy balloony bag. Then
a terrible high-up **waiiiiiiii** came from
the pipes.

'Hiss!' **Pounce! Pop! Waiiiii** . . .

59

'Oh, Wilbur, you've squashed it!' said Winnie. 'What did you do that for? I'll have to try another ninstrument.' Winnie held her wand end on to her lips.

'Abracadabra!'

In an instant, Winnie had a shiny trumpet in her hands.

'Lovely! I'll do a fanflare!'

Winnie blew.

No noise came out.

Wilbur smiled. He relaxed.

Winnie scowled and blew a raspberry down the trumpet. **Paaarp!** **Paaarp-paaarp!**

Wilbur pulled a cushion over his head.

PAAAARP! went Winnie.

'Mrrrow!' wailed Wilbur.

'Oh, blooming heck, Wilbur! Perhaps I should try something quieter. Perhaps a stringy thingy ninstrument.' Winnie waved her wand like a bow.

'Abracadabra!'

And there was a violin. Winnie lifted the violin to her chin, then she began to stroke the bow over the strings—

screeeeech.

'Mrrrow-ow-ow!' screeched Wilbur, even louder.

'You'll have to go outside!' said Winnie. 'I can't learn a ninstrument with you making that kind of a racket! Out you go and leave me to perfectify my music-playing in time for school!'

Winnie threw Wilbur out. Slam! She shut the door on him.

'**Squeak-tee-hee!**' laughed the mice who were peeping around corners. They'd been sniffing that cheese, but not daring to come out while Wilbur was there. Now . . .

'**Squeak!**' **Sniff-sniff! Scuttle-scuttle!**

Out came mice from every corner and crevice of the house.

'Go away!' said Winnie as one scuttled over her foot. 'Get off!' Winnie kicked.

'Squeak!' went the mouse.

'Oh!' said Winnie. 'That was a nice little sound!' She gently poked another mouse with her wand.

'Squeak!'

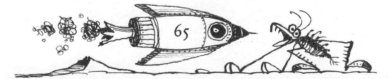

'What a lovely low squeak!' she said.
'Hmm. I've just had a blooming good idea!'

Winnie tiptoed to the door and quietly
opened it. **Creeeeak!** 'Wilbur!' she
whispered. 'Come back inside and catch
some mice for me, but don't hurt them!'

In came Wilbur. Soon he'd got eight
different-sized mice, and put them in a box.

'Right,' said Winnie. 'Time to go off to
the school!'

In the school hall all the little ordinaries
sat nice and quiet, waiting to see what Winnie
had in her box. So did the teachers. So did
Mrs Parmar. Up went one small hand.

'What kind of an instrument is it?'

'It's a mouse organ!' said Winnie. 'Shall
I show you?'

'Yes please!' shouted all the little
ordinaries.

So Winnie opened the box. She tipped
out the mice. The mice looked a bit shy.
Winnie put them in size order, then she
gave one a gentle prod with her finger.

'**Squeak!**' went the mouse.

Giggle! went the children.

Winnie poked another. '**Squeak!**'
And another. '**Squeak!**'

'Um . . . is that it?' asked Mrs Parmar.
'Just mice squeaking?'

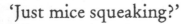

'Er . . .' said Winnie. But Wilbur was handing her her wand.

'Oh, no!' said Mrs Parmar, holding up a hand. 'Absolutely no magic in front of the children!'

'I was only going to conduct the mice with my baton,' said Winnie.

'Oh, very well, then,' said Mrs Parmar.

Winnie raised her wand. She pretended to cough but she was actually cough-whispering, *'Abracadabra!'*

And instantly . . .

'We are eight little mice

Squeak-squeak!

Who live in Winnie's hice

Squeak-squeak!

And sing very nice.

In winter when it's cold
If we're feeling bold
We'll slide down the ice-icles.
Squeak-squeak!

In summer when it's hot
We really like a lot
To ride on our bice-icles.
Squeak-squeak!'

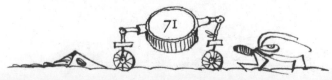

The children laughed and clapped, and
they were soon singing and squeaking
along too. The teachers were delighted.

'Phew in a shrew stew!' said Winnie to
Wilbur as they left the school. 'And
nobody noticed the magic, did they?'

Back home, they opened up the box of mice, and now, instead of Winnie feeling cross with the mice and Wilbur feeling greedy for the mice, they felt all soppy about the mice.

'Shall we all share some cheese?' said Winnie.

'Meeow,' nodded Wilbur.

So the mice joined them for a pongy cheese party before they all settled into bed.

'Sweet cheesy dreams, everyone!' yawned Winnie. Then they all lay awake all night.

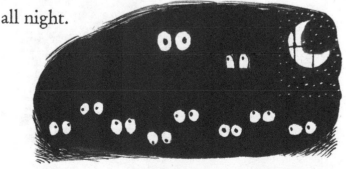

WINNIE

takes the Plunge

Gurgle! went Winnie's loo. **Gurgle-wurgle!**

Winnie pulled the handle again, but it wouldn't flush! It just went **belch-burp!**

'Oh, leaping loo rolls!' said Winnie. 'There's something wrong with this blooming loo, and I don't know what to do about it!'

'Meeow?' suggested Wilbur, waving a plunger.

'It's worth a try!' agreed Winnie.
Splish-splosh! Squirt! Squelch!
went the plunger. Winnie pulled the
handle again. **Burp!** went the loo.
'There's something down there!' said
Winnie. 'Something getting in the way!'
She leant over the loo, peering deep down
into the bowl. 'Pull the handle, Wilbur,
and I'll see if I can see what's blocking it.'

Yank! went Wilbur on the handle.
And **flush-swoosh!** went the loo.

'Ahhhh!' went Winnie as she was
flushed down the pan.

'Mrrow!'

Wilbur tried to hold on to Winnie's
legs. But the pent-up flush was so fierce it
swept Winnie down and away.

'Meeeow!' cried Wilbur. 'Meow, meow!' But the loo was empty. Winnie was gone. 'Meeow!' wailed Wilbur in a voice he hadn't used since he was a kitten.

Down the pipes Winnie was whizzing—**whoops! whoops!**—just as if she was going down a flume at the swimming pool. Except this pipe was dark. This pipe was smelly. This pipe went on and on . . .

Gasp! went Winnie, coming up for
air but still swishing along. 'What the
blooming . . . ?' Something slimy and
wiggly was swimming along with her.
'Who in the loo are you? Are you the
loo-blocking critter?' said Winnie. She gave
the critter a good poke with her wand as
she struggled on down the pipe.

Winnie was running out of energy for
swimming. Help! thought Winnie.
Splashing and gurgling, she just about
managed to wave her wand. If you've tried
waving anything under water you'll know
that it isn't as easy as it is in the air. But
Winnie pushed her wand in a slow swish.
'Abra-gurgle-cadabra!' And instantly
Winnie's legs were transformed into
a mermaid tail!

She waggled her tail, and shot-swam through the water.

'Wheee!' said Winnie. And—**sploosh!**—out she squirted from the pipe into clear cold salty water that glittered brightly in the sunshine. Wiggle-waggle went Winnie's tail, pushing her upwards towards air and light and . . .

'Where the blooming heck am I?' said soggy Winnie.

'You, my dear, are in Merland!' said a deep voice. And there in the water beside Winnie was a handsome merman, flipping his handsome tail.

'Oooer!' said Winnie. 'Er . . . could you tell me which direction is home, please?'

'Certainly! You will come home with me, my dear!' said the merman. 'You can be my merwife!' And he placed a string of pearls around Winnie's neck.

'Ooo, no. No thank you!' said Winnie.
'But I am strong and brave. You must
marry me!' The merman took hold of
Winnie's arm.

Winnie bopped the merman on the
head with her wand, but he snatched it
from her. 'Let go, you blooming bully!'
said Winnie. 'Anyway, I bet you're not as
brave as my Wilbur is! He'll be here soon.'

'Wilbur?' said the merman. 'Is Wilbur your big brother?'

'No! He's my cat!' said Winnie. 'He'll be coming to rescue me, I'm sure. Look! I think that's him now!'

Now, if there's one thing fishy people are scared of, it's cats. 'I'm off!' said the merman, and away he dived.

A small dot on the horizon was getting bigger as it got closer. 'Wilbur!' shouted Winnie. Wilbur was on an old plank, trying to paddle with a wooden spoon. 'Oh, Wilbur, you're as brave as twenty mermen! Take me home, Wilbur!'

Winnie powered the raft through the water with her wonderful tail.

'This tail is brillaramaroodles for swimming,' said Winnie. 'But when we get home I'm going to need to magic my legs back.' But just then . . . 'Whoops!' Winnie was caught up in a fisherman's net and hauled aboard his boat.

'Mrrrow!' protested Wilbur.

'Oi!' shouted Winnie.

But the fisherman had his iCod on and didn't hear a thing.

When they reached the harbour,
Winnie was thrown into a van with the
other fish. Wilbur clung to the back as
they drove to the fish shop. But he
couldn't stop Winnie from being
dumped onto the counter.

87

'Meeow!' said Wilbur, as Winnie
floundered with the flounders and the chip
shop man beat up his batter. 'Meeeow!'

'Throw some fish heads to that noisy
cat!' said the fish-and-chip shop man.

Wilbur kept banging on the window and
pointing, but, 'I'm not giving you that big
cross fish, if that's what you're after!'
laughed the fish-and-chip shop man.

The man peeled the potatoes to make
chips, and he lit the stove. It wouldn't
be long before he began cooking the fish.
So, as fast as a blast, Wilbur ran to Jerry's
house. There he told Scruff . . .

'Meeow meow-meow!'

'Ruff-woof!' agreed Scruff.

Then Scruff told Jerry, so Jerry came
running, with Scruff and Wilbur trying
to keep up, all the way back to the
fish-and-chip shop.

Jerry stomped into the fish shop.
'I wants a giant-sized fish and
chips, please!'

'*Giant-sized?*' said the fish-and-chip
shop man.

'Aha! We do have an exceptionally large fish in the catch today. I'll just pop it into the fryer.'

'No!'

'Mrrrow!'

'Woof!'

'Er . . . I likes my fish raw,' said Jerry.

'Really?' said the fish-and-chip shop
man. 'Well, that saves me a job!' He piled
a mountain of chips onto a huge bit of
paper, then he plonked Winnie on top
of the chips.

'Fanks!' said Jerry. His fish-and-chip
parcel was wriggling and saying rude
things. So he sat on some grass and
unwrapped his supper. His 'fish' had her
hands on her hips.

'Why didn't you stop him from showering me in blooming salt and vinegar?' asked Winnie. 'I feel as sour and as salty as a pickled bunion!'

But Winnie soon cheered up, scoffing chips. And Wilbur ran home to fetch a spare wand. Winnie waved it. *'Abracadabra!'*

93

And instantly her legs were back.

'Oo, that's blooming better!' said
Winnie. 'Legs are useful!'

They walked home as the sun set.

'I'll mend your loo, if you like,'
offered Jerry.

'Oo, would you?' said Winnie.

So Jerry brought his mallet, and
smash!—that was the end of the
problem loo.

94

'But now we haven't got *any* loo!' said
Winnie. 'Heck, where's that wand?
Abracadabra!'

And there was a pair of loos. His and
hers. Winnie and Wilbur pulled down a
handle each.

Flush! Flush! No problem.

'Hoo-blooming-ray' said Winnie.

95

Enjoy more magic moments with
Winnie AND **Wilbur**